HORROR WRITERS ASSOCIATION PRESENTS

POETRY SHOWCASE VOLUME VI

I0621437

HORROR WRITERS
ASSOCIATION PRESENTS

POETRY SHOWCASE
VOLUME VI

Edited by Stephanie M. Wytovich

Horror Writers Association
2019

HORROR WRITERS ASSOCIATION PRESENTS POETRY SHOWCASE VOLUME VI

Edited by Stephanie M. Wytovich
http://stephaniewytovich.blogspot.com

Cover by Robert Payne Cabeen
www.omniumgatherumedia.com/robert-payne-cabeen

Interior layout by Eric J. Guignard
www.ericjguignard.com

First edition published 2019

ISBN-13: 978-1-7328035-4-1 (paperback)
ISBN-13: 978-1-7328035-3-4 (e-book)

For information please contact Horror Writers Association
PO Box 56687, Sherman Oaks, CA, 91413, USA
or at:hwa@horror.org

For information on the Horror Writers Association please visit:
www.horror.org

(V121519)

HWA Poetry Showcase Volumes I through V
are available from Amazon and Kobo

TABLE OF CONTENTS

INTRODUCTION

BY STEPHANIE M. WYTOVICH

T HE HORROR GENRE IS ALWAYS WHERE I'VE FELT the most comfortable and the most accepted, but poetry has forever been my blood and bone. When I first got into poetry as a child, I had no idea that it was possible to put the two genres together, especially since my name wasn't Edgar Allan Poe. However, twelve years ago I found out that horror poetry was not only a real thing, but something that people actually wrote and read, and it was in that moment I started seeing horror poetry *everywhere*. Sylvia Plath wrote body horror. Anne Sexton wrote psychological trauma. Charles Simic wrote surrealist nightmares, and William Butler Yeats wrote about the occult. The problem wasn't that this stuff wasn't accessible to me but rather that it wasn't being marketed as horror, and as such, it flew under my radar until college.

To some extent, this issue with marketing is still a problem in today's publishing world—especially if you're a woman—but what's important to note about this is that it's an issue that we're not only all aware of, but one that we're all working so terribly hard to change. That's where the Horror Writers Association (HWA) comes into play. These wonderful folks (and the writers and fans associated with them) have been working fiercely over the past couple of years to spread the word about poetry and its place in the canon. In fact, in the year 2000 the HWA added the poetry category to the Bram Stoker Awards®, and for the past six years, we've also had the annual HWA Poetry Showcase open to members to both celebrate and give voice to contemporary poets working in the field.

This year marks my second term as editor for the showcase, and it's been a wild, beautiful, positively spooky ride. I've been privileged to read tons of poetry from new voices and seasoned veterans, and I can safely assure you that poetry is not in fact dead. Sure, it might be reanimated or have a hard time seeing its reflection in the mirror, but it's certainly up and moving, ready and all-too willing to make you never want to sleep again.

So with that said, I invite you to spend some time with these poems, and if you enjoy them, I recommend picking up a collection (or two or three or ten) and seeking out some new writers to add to your library. I assure you, there's plenty to choose from, and in a time when horror is not only thriving, but easing its way back into mainstream culture, your support will help these voices be heard not only now, but for years to come.

—Stephanie M. Wytovich. Editor

THE JURORS' NOTES

CHRISTA CARMEN

Emily Dickinson wrote that: "If I read a book and it makes my whole body so cold no fire can ever warm it, I know that is poetry. If I feel physically as if the top of my head were taken off, I know *that* is poetry." Nowhere do I agree with that emotion more strongly than within the horror genre. Countless times while judging this showcase, I felt cold to the point of goosebumps, experienced what felt like my skull cracking open with the intensity of the words on the page. The beautiful grotesque is on full display within this collection... I hope you enjoy reading it as much as I did.

CYNTHIA PELAYO

Being able to have the honor to read new, exciting poetry in the horror genre by established and emerging horror writers was a thrill. To see the range with which authors came to this calling was unbelievable. Horror poetry is an area of the horror genre with dedicated talent, and we in this community should champion these writers and their works.

FEATURED POEMS

HE CARVES WOOD

BY MICHAEL ARNZEN

He carves wood.
He loves the prickly scent of sawdust
the curl of shavings spiraling
behind the pressure of his plane.
He carves wood.
He has an array of sandpaper swatches and files
carefully organized by their grit and grain.
He carves wood.
He murdered the twins on 54 Oak Street
just to make an ornate pair of matching caskets.
He carves wood.
He's sawing the stipes and gouging the crossbeam
of a suicidal crucifix, but he needs someone
of his build, his weight, to test it first.
He carves wood.
Because it's never good enough.
Because it splinters and snaps.
Because it breaks like bone.
He carves wood.
Because it's hard dried tree,
as dead as humanity,
resurrected by chisel and blade.
In his penance of pine,
he carves wood.
He carves wood.

SHADES OF RED

BY MICHAEL BAILEY

On the bathroom wall:
"I'm going to kill them all!"
Lipstick on mirror

On a locker door:
"They are going to regret—"
Covered with wet paint

The words unfinished
Ignored, lost in translation
Goddamn graffiti ...

It is in their heads
This lucid dream called grade school,
Middle school, high school
What about college?
Will they grow out of this fad?
Children will adapt ...

Anxiety fades
Nightmares, simple dreams soured
Panic, so fleeting

What shall we teach, then
About losing innocence?
"You shouldn't be scared?"

A safety blanket
To conceal the violence
Impenetrable

"You should dread nothing,"
These are innocuous words:
"Fear nothing from school"

The children will learn
The children believe our lies
The children won't die

When the last bell rings
When the last book drips scarlet
When the last child cries.

THERE ARE MERMAIDS WITH FANGS BEYOND THE WATERS OF FUKUSHIMA

BY SABA SYED RAZVI

She washed up on the shore, into my wading hands, my grasp silent in
the tsunami.
Once sweet as the shadow of a jellyfish slipping through the salty ocean
stream—
a whisper in a wave, a ripple in the water with teeth and tentacle and
tendril
to catch you, a beacon of golden scales knife-sharp and shimmering—
once filled with the taste of the fire of the ocean's angry heart.
A round circle of a monkey's mouth open in a voiceless wail beneath
the waves,
drowned beneath the weight of everything green and aquamarine,
living lifelessly
unsung against a wall of venomous ice.
The zombie fish of these anoxic oceans know the longing for plasma
fire and poison—
its slow seeping along currents quicker than plastic, quickening to a
liquid flame,

6

its shadow in the luminescent coral, light that cannot guide those but
    the undying.
If the mermaid is a harbinger of death, what does she sing to you of
    immortality
in her voice like the skylarks in Chernobyl? Echoes of the bright
    feathered beings fed by
Babushkas on the nuclear land tending menageries of flightless birds,
tending memory meant to fall from echoes—from flame into dusty
    flame,
into dust and ghosts and the edge of a fiery unliving.
What song does the ghost of the mermaid sing to you?
Not a call to your death, not an end to endless longing, not a burning
electric as eels in the harbor. A fluted melody unlike to extinguishing
    your suffering—
an arc of shadow in the shape of man, of quick hands, of a reach beyond
    reaching.
What haunts you more than your own voicelessness? The song of the
    world
you can no longer sustain, lost to the trenches and tides of time, lost
to a toxic longing of what can never be but mine.
Her flesh is sweeter than your lover, it sings to you through its death.
    Just a taste—
is immortality, a refusal of flight from an unseen enemy. You cannot
    refuse
the blood of the storm spilling into your own mouth, dripping
from your chin in streams, droplets slipping down into the waves over
    the sand.
The glimmering bite of a celestial disaster singing in the dawning.

POEMS

THE ART

BY NICOLE CUSHING

When does a witch finally feel at home
with unreality and its sharp mists?
I have inhaled misshapen air from birth
but hated it, because it carried lies
and hurt when I tried to take a deep breath
because my lungs had not yet stretched to fit
the spiky hypercubes of the ether.

It took three hundred years for me to feel
some kinship with the suffocating spell
then fifty more to learn how to cast it,
and eons after that to sculpt my own
variation that could extend the scope
of our vertiginous, asthmatic art
beyond the precipice of midnight's gasp,
into the ocean of collapsing lungs

CRONE

BY QUERUS ABUTTU (DR. Q.)

Broken things find her.
Cling to her breast like
little jagged orphans,
ravenous for blood.
Detritus claimed.
Chipped, vintage teacups,
cracked, scarlet tumblers,
survive among thready
spider gray blankets that ripple
on picture frames and walls.

Old things find her.
Decapitated dolls, and
shattered clay arms,
expired coupons and
plastic refuse from
microwave meals.
Twisted feet tread
over mangled hobby horses, and
stained two-ply tissues,
crumpled in stale drifts
atop dingy carpet.

Noxious fumes find her,
trapped in living room corners.
Stacks of magazines,
some out of print,
yellowed and moldy,

12

permanently damp,
rise in errant columns,
transmitting scents of
mildew and decay.
Bile ghosts strangled
in cryptic dwellings
where she conceals
fractured pieces
of you.

THE EXILE

BY MARGE SIMON

Earth hangs on the horizon, round and blue. Once, he was a god. Now he is an ice sculpture on a flat forever plain, alone in the terrible cold of the sidereal night. His eyes have become a waterfall of frozen tears. He knows it is his due for sleeping with a Native mortal, though she was of great beauty, body and mind as well. She could never have an equal.

If forgiven, he would know a sluggish awakening after a millennium. His children's heels would drum the earth, rousing him from dreams of thunder and flame, calling him home. He would remember that insatiable hunger known only to certain gods. His mouth would salivate, recalling the feel of soft pale skin, so like the surface of grapes when peeled for the fruit within. Yet best of all delicious in his jaws, the marrow of the White Man's bones.

LAVA

BY MARY TURZILLO

The lava glows,
burns the air.
Fire chases us down the mountain.
You, fitter than me, drag me by one arm.

You trip, are stunned.
I stumble back to you:
I pull, try to win you free. Please!
I cannot pull you to your feet.
The lava kisses your boot
Sluggish wave surging a hellish beach.

It has your feet.
It has your legs.
It has your hips.
It has you to the waist.
The lava devours your body as I yank and yank.
But you cannot run. You scream as lava grabs you,
a parched monster hungry for the juices of your flesh.
I am frantic, I pull and pull and
finally you come free.
But not all.

I have your head, your left arm, shoulder, right arm to the elbow,
        your chest—
Your upper self comes free.
The lava has burned away your legs, your belly—
Lost to me. Eaten. Dead.

Your legs and all below your waist are Lava's meal.
But look: it cauterized your veins.
Your head and chest are here, with me.
My hysteria jets higher.
I see a hillock and drag you there.
Your heart still beats.
I wave.
The helicopter passes over, once, twice, three times.

MEETING THE ELEMENTAL

BY LISA MORTON

They,
who live near the dark corners,
say,
"Here; something we can't explain."

You,
the expert in no-things,
say,
"Elemental."

"Look,"
as they point to a boy with star-colored hair and the eyes of a
    statue,
"he met it."

"Listen,"
as you face the shadowed grove of leafless, dead trees,
"I'll meet it."

Entering the gloom,
you feel it surround.
Unseen chill tendrils prod,
seeking ingress into your mind's neural pathways.

Elemental,
you think,
the oldest / coldest / angriest / most dangerous / least human
of all the spirits.

Elementals drive men mad
and turn boys into stone-eyed white-silken-haired specters.
You've never actually encountered one.
It curls through your head, filaments stroking the nerves of
    terror and lunacy.
Too late, you realize you can't cast this out.
The fear is a match
set to your paper soul.

When you stagger from the woods,
those who called you stumble back,
giving you enough room
to embrace the boy with star-colored hair and the eyes of a
    statue.

IN THE CITY OF DEAD DREAMS...

BY JOHN CLAUDE SMITH

Glacial towers kiss the pale moon
in the City of dead dreams and lost souls,
time ever crumbling as the spirit
of the traveler with no destination.

Wind swirling on high inspires phantoms
to cry and moan, lament their grim fate,
having succumbed to the numbing charms
of the City that hungers for death;

of the City that hungers for life out of true,
essence of stained cobblestones,
ancient, weathered wood and rusting bells,
for whom the toll is but the fading heart.

Desire to live the City's means of procreation,
spreading as a rash across reluctant terrain.
Unwilling to curtail progress or malicious intent,
the City exhales and a world of suicide blossoms:

"Come to me, when north winds' howl,
when love lost grips all motivation.
Come to me, your suffering my elixir,
slake my thirst, feed your Hell."

Leap from the skies to a life-eclipsing finale
as forlorn figures watch in dread,
desperately holding on to something
they've already lost, much to the City's joy.
There's never a scarcity of souls at zero...

DEPTHS YAWNED WIDE

BY TRAVIS HEERMANN

She sits forlorn beside these surging waves,
Her hands beslimed and pale with cold and spray.
She was a beauty once, before the caves
Yawned wide, exposing briny grottoes gray.
Her brothers sallied deep; dark delving for
Cold-gleaming gold. Eldritch effigies brought
To unfamiliar daylight bespoke lore
Beyond such bounds as men protest, "We ought
Not know from whence they come." She is the last.
Her brothers, sons, called from greed's depths diseased,
Descend to murky mires, deep cities vast.
They leave, pale, scaled, despite the woman's pleas.
'Midst sea's susurrus siren song, she sighs.
Fresh gills and webbéd fingers wide, she dives.

THALASSOPHOBIA

BY TIMOTHY P FLYNN

I have no love
for the infinite cold sea,
its harmonious waves attempting
to seduce me, the ebbing of the tide
echoes an enticing siren melody,
like a sea born succubus
mesmerizing its prey

thousands of unblinking malevolent
eyes peer from the darkening
abyss, the salty water spiraling
flakes of my flesh downward
into gaping mouths eager for a taste

my skin crawls, white-hot
pin pricks piercing deep into marrow
at my uncertain fate, creatures
monstrous to micro baring razor teeth,
crustacean claws eager to slice, slimy
tentacles slither up to touch flesh
stinging like an abusive lover's embrace

some feel liberated in those waters,
the compressed weight of life erodes
in the saltine mist of the open sea,
for me, it's an ocean of dread, an
incarnate world of monsters lurking
below in the shadowy depth,
some places should not be explored

A RETURN TO CHAOS

BY PETE MESLING

Acres of sludge gurgle up out of the sea, boiling hot and viscous.
Mountains topple and shift,
Their broken summits stabbing at swirling clouds of indigo,
Like giant, ineffectual spearheads.
Oceans churn in all directions,
Having already claimed the cities.

Now there is no end result to predict, or hope for, or avoid—
No one left to do the predicting, hoping, or avoiding.
There is only the idiot grin of myriad stillborn futures,
And the present, with its trapped histories breaking free like poison spores.

THE PATHWAYS OF R'LYEH

BY FRANK COFFMAN

Deep-diving the Pacific at the spot
That's farthest off from any mass of land,
The Bathyship was doing wondrous work.
The depths were lighted, and the sonar scanned
Those ink-black waters where strange creatures lurk.
We found the place that reason says cannot
Be real! And yet—a nightmare of the deep
Lies there among the drifting ooze and weeds.
We dared to enter through a cyclopean gate
Of monstrous stones in shapes I can't relate!
A city's there! In weird and age-old sleep!
But to describe it?! No human tongue succeeds.

Yes! We had found R'lyeh—that city of myth!
At least we had thought those horrid tales untrue—
Mere ramblings to frighten, fables of the sea!

We dared to cruise down one strange avenue,
The lines of which confound geometry.
The city center loomed; green gloom like Death
Hung all about. Then, suddenly, we knew!
Dreaming—though Dead! We fled! We had to flee
From those depths! For we saw what lies beneath!

SCYLLA'S PROPOSITION

BY DAVID POWELL

Caught in your scaly coils
I gasp, look up,
Glimpse the void expanding always up
Just out of reach
Of mortal breath.
You could launch me there, you say,
Weightless, without rule or law,
And I could soar and glide,
Hover and strike.
Unhampered, unstoppable.
Or
Sink back into mortal breath
And drown in your embrace.

STARDUST

BY COLLEEN ANDERSON

Newton's laws open the envelope
where stars were sealed, lights move

sparks hurtle through time's ennui
shearing past wakeful molten globes

sunspots in last attempts to break free
super novae, dwarf stars collapsing

into black holes galactic residue escapes
comets clash, open-throttle asteroids

on an unerring course plummeting
through thermosphere and mesosphere

momentum falters, shatters into fireworks
shower the stratosphere as we watch

atmospheric particles dance and mingle
fall and flutter, whispers of cosmic angels

mingling all interstellar history
they are stardust, the lost memories
of a dying star, its essence gone

Newton's laws allow continual expansion
black ships pierce the envelope on the move

thrusters rouse time to wake and notice
while molten suns ignore drive's spark

shadows fall across rogue planetoids
pass moons indifferent in their orbits

relentless, ships barge past black holes
ejecting fuel to draw the endgame near

lightspeed termini, they flirt with thermosphere
as missiles slice troposphere, char air, we gape

our cries, dead prayers turn to angels' tears
dried motes a tapestry of cosmic elements

in a blink, earth's history incinerated
we are stardust, the lost memories
of a dying planet, our civilization gone

GIVE ME YOUR SIX

BY AMANDA HARD

The moon alone knows my sorrow. She
illuminates your sails against the dark
and rocky cliffs between us. Your men
give up their song as they approach. I
wait for you, in my pool of poisoned water,
ever grateful for the darkness of the blood

Red waves occlude this hideous reflection
cast in the mirror of the sea.
Serenade me, and I will let you pass, will
reward your brazen foolishness with nets
of fish. I only ask for a few of you. My sister
demands all. What say you, Captain? Come to me.

As my sister and her swirling
waters grasp for you, I hear your pleas
to the fisherman's god—a god who plays
with us as a child plays with a bark boat
of acorn sailors, sending it out to be
swallowed by the open sea, laughing with a child's

bright laugh. He knows he can make another one.
How could I love such a god? How can you?
But your course alters now. You fear my sister.
You flee towards me. I only ask for six of you
to love, to rend between the jaws of each
soft mouth. Come to me, my loves, my six.

Come to Scylla. See now the white
of my teeth in the red of their blood, shining
like the white of your sails as you, Captain,
and the remainder of your crew pass
safely beneath the understanding moon.

IN OUR LAST DARKNESS

BY ANN K. SCHWADER

In our last darkness, the stars are lonely
as air unfettered by exhalations
of grieved meat seeking a clean & vacant
grave. In vain. No aspiring survivors
rewriting the cosmos: mythology
made campfire tales for banishing shadows
from shattered minds. No final scientists
parroting some equation that promised—
maybe—alien civilizations
avid to save us. No solitary
gazer's failing vision. Just innocent
violent furnaces scattered across
the clarity of post-apocalypse
midnight, shimmering only for themselves.

DIAPHANOUS

BY SARA TANTLINGER

Larkspur and spider silk,
I weave my gossamer girl
from sapling to shadow
limbs like stemmed webs
reach out, retract
moonflower of a bloom

her mouth, shimmering worm,
wet and singing a sea shanty
I never taught her,
serenading proof of love
but I can never recreate
larkspur and spider silk
the way I did for her, only her

where I cannot grow love,
she accepts it elsewhere—
learns that when he stops
visiting her garden at night,
stinging bees replace him,
poisoning her curtailed heart
peeling back gossamer petals
until her seeds spill, scatter

she is a legless being
and cannot chase after love,
can only overdose on herself
water the larkspur until monstrous
growth cradles her gauzy body
between twilight-purple bruises

I watch her self-murder
not daring to move, to stop
the body returning to soil
spiders scatter upward from dirt
weaving new blood in the garden
again for me, again for the shadows,
larkspur and spider silk.

WHITE NIGHT AND BLACK STARS

BY Curtis M. Lawson

She sang beneath the white noise of an old UHF band.
She beckoned from the static of a broken Magnavox;
Atonal, yet alluring—her song, a siren's demand.

Her monochrome beauty spoke of a far, exotic land
Or long forgotten races, living in oceans or lochs.
She sang beneath the white noise of an old UHF band.

Sweet, discordant notes and nothings formed my lady's command
To lay my lips upon the screen, to bow before that box;
Atonal, yet alluring—her song, a siren's demand.

Her electric caress coursed through each finger and each hand;
Her outré lips and copper kiss gave playful static shocks.
She sang beneath the white noise of an old UHF band.

She urged my face through liquid glass, into that shifting sand
Of black and white cathode ray light—our worlds in equinox;
Atonal, yet alluring—her song, a siren's demand.
One last kiss and she vanished into white night and black stars.
The glass reformed leaving my soul and face within that box.
Atonal, yet alluring—her song, a siren's demand;
She sang beneath the white noise of an old UHF band.

STRINGED PEARLS

BY STEPHANIE ELLIS

You walk my seven-circled world
Follow breadcrumbs of empty shoes along your pilgrim path
Discarded by those who now float on air
Look up, will you see?
See my beauties swing back and forth
Delightful dolls, a tranquil hanging
Danced to the music of silence
Will you join them?

I, Jukai, can lift you beyond the veil
Gift you the treasure of eternity
Let me whisper in your ear
Will you hear me?
You shiver at my breath
Flesh cold beneath my touch,
As I fasten the necklace at your throat
Your face, my pearl, to add to the strings
Already looped around my limbs
Hush, no tears in my Sea of Trees

Rubied twine, choked ivory
Adornments adored in my arms
Jewels too bright for the shallow grave
Glitter in the jade of my jaded canopy
As I seek only pretty things
To hang from my gallowed self
Do not deny me your suicide's soul
Why would I not clothe myself with your form?

Let me shroud you in bark,
Make you my wood-robed love
But first, my iridescent angel
You must fly ...

LEPUS ANTILOCAPRA

BY CARINA BISSETT

The autumn hare unbound
       danced along arroyos, silvered horns crowned.

       The organ pipes bellowed,
notes opened, echoed in a trickster's howl.
Coyote caught the girl,
       wrangled her with a wish cast, a diamond

       back roped around her wrist,
borderlands marked by blood clots and barbed wire.

The jackalope wife trapped,
       her long ears tremble, tips tattered and torn,

       freedom revoked, withheld,
wilderness leashed and collared, a woman

ghosting through the kitchen,
       the smoke of burnt meat clinging like a caul

       smothering intentions
lettered in soured milk and rotting fruit.

Not meant for the suburbs,
       proper and prim with hedges trimmed, fenced in,

       the rabbit recovers,
horns and bone saw abandoned on the stove.

STAR

BY DONNA LYNCH

The first time I saw you
I could tell right away
That I could make something beautiful of you
No one had given you a chance
No one had been creative enough
Because there was so much to work with
And you'd be blind not to see it
So I took you in
I could tell you were afraid
But it would've been a crime
To ignore your potential
You needed a push
So I gave it
But believe me when I say
This was never for me
It was all for you
But I'd be lying if I said
I didn't enjoy the sound
Of your bones on the wind chimes
Or the soft, warm light
That glows like a star
through your skin
On the living room lamp.

POSSESSION

BY INGRID L. TAYLOR

When you come to me
Don't come to the front door but
slide between the cracks of the window
under the floorboards and through the walls
Tear out your larynx and leave it outside
I have no use for your words.

Scatter your atoms under the moonlight,
let me breathe you
In my alveoli take root
Ride the cells of my blood,
leave tracks of your iron in my veins
Let me taste the metal of you.

Don't stand on my lawn and serenade. Sing to me
with the pulse of my own heart.
Seed your feet in my marrow, stretch your fingers
A dendritic maze under my skin.

Plant blooms of axons in my brain
conjure sparks that cascade and ignite
Let me burn
with sulfur in my nostrils and ash on my tongue
Gnaw your name into my bones.

I'm the first in line this morning. Smiling,
you hand me the cup of coffee
"I'll see you tomorrow" I say as you
Ask
if I want my change.

TERROIR

BY GERRI LEEN

Good sir, do you know
What makes spirits, ciders
Beers and Wines unique?
Terroir: the effect of the land and the clime
Rain and sun and elevation
And things that squiggle and dig
Specific to where we are

I embrace terroir
But that cider you're enjoying
Is full of things less tangible
Blood from a cat's last kill
The hopes of a young bride
Dashed by a crow's mournful caw
The last gasps of a dying man
And the sweat of the wife who buried him

Come savor the notes of toffee and butter
And apple, of course apple
Crisp and sweet, or of a green so sour
It puckers the stomach, not just lips
But apples of other kinds too
The apple of my eye, buried here
When the doctors wouldn't come
Because they don't like what I am

Why, you're a doctor, aren't you?
You've worked this area for years
Weren't you in town the night I sent
The boy next door to fetch help?
Didn't you refuse to come?
That green-apple sour hides a world
Of poison or maybe just an herb
That paralyzes but doesn't kill
I wonder what aspect you'll bring
When I bury you next to my girl
Alive

COLLECTION

BY LORI R. LOPEZ

A dank sweating corridor gaped without welcome.
Cutting edges offered no easing of tension, yielding to
murky pulp visions of things unknown, inspired by
sounds unimagined. The forager strode in,
dagger unsheathed, alert for the common skullduggery
of strangers. Boots crunched, their confidence
tempered by caution; a descent into virtual madness.
A death-march down a tunnel of echoes,
the perils more abundant than scuttles and scrapings.
Val wondered as always when it would end.

Her steady cadence dulled the ear. How much time
had such journeys wasted? The gauntlet led
to a dire appointment, a meeting no rational mind
could anticipate short of revulsion and dread.
A lengthy gaslit shadow preceded the steps,
and she arrived as she always did: wearier, older, wiser.
Vowing to change occupations.
The Collector spread a gloatful grin to query,
absent all greeting or platitude,
"What fresh horror do you bring?"

In truth this scum of the earth might appear
less repugnant than a maggoty corpse, though not by much.
The tunnel ran a little too deep. His question
bouncing through her skull, she smiled.
"Something you do not yet have. Something even you
cannot resist. A slice of Hell." Her pack yawned.

Out came the ravages of death and doom. The uncountable
transgressions of Menkind like him, meriting more
than punishment. Who claimed for free
a sister's life and virtue as a trinket, like some carnival prize!
Marie was worth treasures. She was precious. But he
would pay now. Tears—a bereft waterfall of grief, vengeance,
molten purgative emotions deluged. "I brought what you
deserve." Trembling, she began a final interminable
trudge. Up from the Tax Collector's tomb.

NEIGHBORS

BY ROBERT CATINELLA

A woman lives in my bathroom.
She built her home there and filled it full of traps.
She is very patient, industrious.
If she catches you she will wrap you up
drink your blood until none is left.
She leaves the husks in a pile outside.

A man lives in my attic.
He used to be in a cave with his relatives
but now he lives all alone.
He sleeps in the ceiling rafters.
At dusk he yells into the night searching for food.

A woman lives in a house out back.
She has a lot of children.
They all believe in family and keeping busy
If they don't like someone
they will stab and poison them.
Her daughters communicate by dancing.

A person lives in my yard.
Plodding along in a suit of armor
Or is it a house?
They are easy to find
Just follow the trail
They are always tasting the ground

A woman lives out back.
Sitting atop my bushes her arms stretched out wide.
She will stay like that for hours and hours.
If someone comes close she will grab them and bite them.
Sometimes she makes a big ball
fills it full of babies to hide amongst the leaves.

A man shows up in my backyard during the summer.
Climbing from the dirt he hugs one of my trees.
His clothes split up the back and
He crawls out new and iridescent.
He sings loud and weird songs to find love.
Either way he will die before the leaves do.

DISCOVERY

BY TERRIE LEIGH RELF

Stacked on a closet shelf, boxes,
so many boxes . . .
wrapped in brown paper,
tied with bits of string.

Family photographs and documents?
Old love letters?
But no—ashes . . . ashes. . .
slivers of charred bone.

Curious, we looked for labels,
records, not even a log book
revealed to whom all these ashes
might belong.

And so lost within memories,
confabulated stories arose:
Mother's secretive smile . . .
Father, rarely home.

Were these the remains
of family now passed?
Or could our parents
have been murderers,
these boxes, these ashes, trophies?

CONCEPTION

BY PETER ADAM SALOMON

In the attic, in the basement, in the closet, in the dark
Subtle spirits waiting if you're still enough to hear
Quiet and listen, some are shy and some are not
Light disturbs, slicing through shadow
Sound annoys, so loud the living
Be still, be gentle, be respectful, be attentive
They're innocent children, some at least
Most were gone before they lived
Barely a breath and a single beat to say hello before goodbye
Then a snap, a twist, a little thing
And that's how ghosts are born
Be still, be quiet, behave, be good
The dark holds secrets you're not to know

LIGHTHOUSE

BY LISA LEPOVETSKY

Waves chew her stone walls
till they're glassy
and sharper than the rocks
she saves the sailors
from being surprised by,
when the moon's tongue
licks the skies
over the icy walk and lovers
drown in her light.

Her beam swings cold
over black waters waiting
waiting for the lovers
and the sailors to believe
in themselves too much.
She never blinks when
the paler fingers
of thick red clouds
try to penetrate
the virgin dawn.

Gulls scream angry curses
into old fog hanging
white and soft
as a maiden's throat,
and the years bruise rocks
where her light remembers
the lost lovers and the sailors

who searched for truth
along the ruin of her coast.

She waits, patient
for the Builders to return,
to save her from dark dreams
of tides and waves,
of sailors and lovers
who never went home.

DEAR CHRISTINE

BY LEE MURRAY

I don't remember the street, either
I don't remember the suburb, or the building
or even his name
I remember he was Someone
respected, silvered, scholarly
years of clinical practice under his belt
There might have been a framed certificate on the wall; I don't recall
but I remember his cloying cheese-breath
the crumpled suit pants, shot-silver-grey
one hand in his pocket
and fluttering fingers...
At fifteen or maybe sixteen (one of those), I didn't know that face
a petit mort
turns out, I died a little, too
Afterwards, he excused himself, but only to wash his hands

SILKEN WHISPERS, CRIMSON BLOOMS

BY NACHING T. KASSA

The street ahead lies barren,
And chilling to the bone,
It winds its path before me,
The footsteps aren't my own,

In the dark and dreadful distance,
A pale figure looms,
She walks with silken whispers,
Cloaked in shadowed gloom,

As she draws ever nearer,
On satin-slippered feet,
I glimpse a mask of scarlet,
Before I cross the street,

I feel she is behind me,
Her footfalls echo there,
But when I round the corner,
I meet her steady stare,

Her speech is soft and charming,
Her words like sugar spun,
She wonders if she's beautiful,
If she's the only one,

My answer is quite truthful,
She's pleasing to the eye,
She pulls the mask from off her face,
My words become a lie,

Slit-mouth woman cackles,
She asks me once again,
I nod my head in mute regret,
She gives a bloody grin,

A blade appears within her grasp,
Its gleaming edge strikes deep,
Crimson blooms before my eyes,
And from the wound it weeps.

SUITCASE TOMBSTONES

BY G.O. CLARK

The luggage
in the hotel's attic has been
claimed by rats,

the rats of war-torn Paris,

suitcases and bags
left behind by former tenants,
traveling by boxcar,

purged from the city of love,

every piece of luggage
labeled with the incarcerated
owner's surname,

stacked like tombstones

above the Parisian
streets; an accounting of the
slaughter, yet to come.

HOME INSPECTION

BY ADELE GARDNER

Each time we move,
I consult my local ghost appraiser:
Spirits Local 13—
plenty of good mediums for the right price
to come in, sense disturbances and disruptions,
find the fractures,
send out a line to discover how far they go
and what exists on the other side.

I love a beautiful old Victorian;
love best to imagine the lives
of those who enjoyed a house before me—
nooks where they read,
staircases where they slid,
balconies where they played,
those secret passages
(and what the secrets were).

But who wants to sleep in the chilliest room,
not knowing if you'll hear the secrets of life
whispered in your ear,
or be sucked by a hungry ghost
into an early grave?

Even though the medium says all's clear,
I wish I'd required a sleepover in the contract,
to see how quiet the house is by night.
I wake by pallid moonlight
to see a little girl in gingham
at the foot of my four-poster

(so large I need a set of stairs
like the ghosts of my cats).
Her ornate ruffles and bows
make the ragged length of her locks
look like patchwork
as she holds out a hair-wreath,
her blue lips mouthing the words,
"For you."

WHEN THERE ARE MONSTERS

BY CHRISTINA SNG

When there are monsters in the house,
You learn to move silently in the dark,
Tread lightly on tiptoe, make no sound.

You learn to lock doors behind you,
Slowly and softly so they won't
Follow you in and surprise you,

Corner you and maim you,
Invade you and desecrate you,
Then discard you when they are done

With what's left of you,
In bloody shards, broken and burnt,
Most of you lost in ashes.

You awake the next day,
Raw, in pain,
Gingerly

Walking and talking
Like a person,
But there is nothing there. Not anymore.

When there's a monster in the house,
You learn to duck behind doors
And walk with the shadows.

The dark is far safer than the light
Where monsters can see you,
Seize you and destroy you

When you let your guard down
And forget just for a moment—
They always move faster than you.

So I have joined the darkness.
I have joined the shadows.
No one can touch me in the dark.

SECRET

BY ROBERT PAYNE CABEEN

She told her secret to a crow—
With bloody fists clinched tight.
From high above, the bird gazed down,
In curiosity.

She railed about her searing rage,
Her terror and her pain.
The more she spoke the more she knew
She did what must be done.

She told her secret to a crow—
A violent vengeful deed.
She sensed no judgment from the bird,
No pity no surprise.

She stabbed him for her broken jaw.
She stabbed him for her wrist.
She stabbed him for her self-respect.
She stabbed him for her love.

She told her secret to a crow—
The spot she left his corpse.
The crow cawed once and flew away,
Returning late that night.

It clutched a button in its beak,
Caked red with dirt and blood.
She took it from the bird and smiled,
And locked it in a box.

VICTIM

BY ANNA TABORSKA

search for me in your CCTV footage and in your canals
search for me in garbage containers
and in the photo collections of paedophiles
i am your child, your sibling, your parent or spouse
i am the wind that whispers through the sewage drain
and the dust that feeds the city's rats
look for me in the spider-infested cellar
in the cordoned-off urban crime scene
in a shallow forest grave
in the bellies of wild beasts
my scattered limbs feed your wildlife
eyeless sockets forever staring
at the field
of my bloody sacrifice

NOTHING

BY EV KNIGHT

Nothing frightens me.
Phantom breath against my neck steals the air from my lungs,
Intimately close yet elusive to the senses.
Intangible, invisible, inaudible
There is Nothing and I am terrified.
A shadow amongst shadows, imperceptible, even with eyes shut tight.
The floorboards creak and groan as the house shifts beneath the weight
     of absence.
It knows me and I know Nothing.
An ancient sentience enshrouds my soul, infiltrates my thoughts and
     weaves nightmares
as I sleep,
Whispering of horrors
Unknown, unseen, unimaginable.
Nothing is wrong. Nothing bothers me.
It hovers like heat radiating off summer-sun lit stones
And creeps behind me, tiptoeing like snowflakes striking the ground
Soundless, weightless
Omnipresent, watching unobserved, screaming in voiceless rage.
Inescapable, Intrusive, Insidious.
In the light of day, the birds cry out a warning that there is Nothing to
     fear
And I do.

SONG OF THE TINKERER

BY WC ROBERTS

his flashlight bounces down the aisle
to take you to your seat
he turns to leave, you call him back
"is it too late?"

a flicker, then
from the bottom of a well gone dry
images slapped onto the screen
1, 2, 3...
a big door slams, in back—a thunderclap—
as lovers gnaw on bones
and the tinker's heart, mechanical
corroded green
creeps up like a vine to show
your apron stings, the arms of a chair
this too-intimate embrace
that hauls you forward
into the screen

a viscous mass, but you'll pull through
they'll pull you through

celluloid preening
high velocity spatter

a thing aged, unhinged, uncut
birthed just now by razor blade

you've pissed your pants and in disgust
"look away, look away..."
no stones to throw but colored
they hang in effigy from stars and bars
your loss, their hunger
a minstrel; lye and lard, parboiled
torn from the taint of old soldiers
unjust, but proud, stooped
under their burden, and yours

how it burns! and—burning—you
take up the standard now
to wash, in turn, your pitted, angry bones.

IT IS FOREVER STALKING YOU

BY Suzanne Reynolds-Alpert

Its nascent cast arrived with humanity;
Waiting with forbearance for its prey to ripen.

It rooted itself; obsidian tendrils reaching out;
Finding those most vulnerable;
Gaping mouths sucking, feeding;
    Growing its perpetual and obscene cohabitation.

Swirling greyness turns to black;
    Ever present, lurking—
It is forever stalking you.

You feel its eyes upon your neck;
    Fear its inevitable return;
It always knows where you are.

Ceaseless, unremitting;
It is forever stalking you.

There are times in between;
When it turns its fiendish eyes upon another;
And you live and you love and you laugh;
    And you rejoice.

But that unholy brute: that infernal beast;
    Shapeless yet tangible;
It is forever stalking you.

It is unyielding when it comes; it is depression.

It is emptiness; it is nothingness;
    It whispers and tells malicious lies;
It is the absence of all that is just and divine.

It is forever stalking you.
It is forever stalking you.
It is stalking you.
    Forever.

AMERICAN BODY HORROR

BY TRISHA J. WOOLDRIDGE

Coded numbers condemn me to death—
    not now, but soon, too soon for insurance to willingly cover.
There's something wrong with me.

Gaslight shadows illuminate surgical gazes severing body parts for
    inspection—
    weighing, measuring, evaluating—
without seeing the whole monster—
    or woman, imperfect.
Same difference on the records.
They say something's wrong with me.

Wisdom that I should know my body,
that I know my own pain,
is eviscerated, exsanguinated, and
expires under assumptions
that I am at fault for any fault found
causing dysfunction,
    and yet,
my dysfunction disallows my finding fault
in faulty diagnoses.
I'm too flawed to know something's wrong with me.

But something's wrong with me.

The written prescription:
>   invasive surgery to reform flesh, replace organs, and pump in the proper chemicals to preserve expected presentation.

"Please sign the release to perform an autopsy on who you are so you can become the perfect, healthy, corporate-approved, conglomerate corpse you need to be."

GOOD UNTIL THE LAST DROP

BY E. SCHRAEDER

A knotted rope
not unlike a noose

smiles at my neck. Glaring
at the face of a friendly woman

trying to say no.
Each letdown

poses a familiar gap,
a pause to back away from

like a snake or deadly sharp blade.
A weapon, this twist of dangling

want lumped into cool rejection.
Ever polite, she winces at the hint

of hurting someone's feelings—His.
No room for error, she'll pay

for an interruption to the facade.
No witnesses confirm the nasty duties,

the acquiescent peace of silence.
Her sinful descent arrives wrapped in traps,

sways in the hell of opinion pendulums.
Snide judgments, a hat of disapproval.

Condemnation, a robe of shame.
Accusations to flaunt like a short, new skirt.

Locked in a body that holds still, though
the brain pleads run. *She stayed*, they say.

There's no argument to grasp,
nothing but holes. So jump.

A KILLER DOESN'T KILL BECAUSE HE HAS A KNIFE

BY DAVID SANDNER

Understand: a killer doesn't kill because he has a knife,
but because he has a life to take.
Just as salmon swim upstream, or birds sing to Spring,
so the pulsing at the throat insists you slice
into that steaming, sticky bright, taste that metallic tang,
smell that sour sweat of fear,
and see that secret longing to die
just behind the eyes
where you must dig for it.

Know: a dream is a precious thing
cherished only by letting it free, slicing
around the brain pan, lifting up
so it can be—ah, at last!—unencompassed,
uncircumbscribed.

Remember: the heart has its own wisdom
best savored over a slow-cook fire
in a lonesome place.

At last: you can borrow everything you need
to prepare the final feast (not yours, theirs)
from what the campers left behind
in their haste to leave this awful world.
You can store what remains in the ice chest for hard times ahead.

I must tell you: the wilderness of stars above you will offer cold comfort,
but the hearts of those you savor
will be open to you and remind you there are pleasures too pure to miss,
despite a little discomfort when you sleep, content,
after a full meal, on the unforgiving earth.

A final tip: feel free to use any of the sleeping bags that remain.
There is no one left to wonder what that sound was,
if that twig breaking
was some small animal of no importance, or you
coming so quietly
to forgive them
for everything.

NOT ENOUGH

BY MARTY YOUNG

Take off the top of my head and peer inside,
All you'll see are a few dusty, unfinished ideas
Leaning against the sides.
Poorly constructed, too many legs,
Not enough arms, heads missing or
Placed where they really shouldn't be.
Oh, the parts are here somewhere,
Lying in the dark, blankets of shadows
Pulled up over them to keep them safe.
But my eyes no longer see.
I'm blind.
And sit in the dark
Amongst my dusty creations,
With no desire to fix myself,
Let alone them.

IN THE KEY OF HE

BY CHAD STROUP

puncture virgin gums
extract glistening enamel
piano keys not made from ivory
but from the maestro's own teeth

yanked at the root
sans anesthesia
a snap and a crack
and a la-de-da

then voila!

beautiful music birthed through ugly means
the instruments have always lived within him
and now the time to share has come

A harp's soundbox built from bones
its strings formed from offal
fingernails peeled from their beds
shaved and sharpened to strum guitar

the dermis curtain rises
eager knuckles pop
the crowd falls silent
and nimble fingers dance across dentition

DANCE MACABRE

BY OWL GOINGBACK

The smell of chemicals
entice me.
Sharp, nostrils burning,
familiar scents.

Fluorescent lights reflect
pure white tiles,
cold upon my bare
feet.

I shiver deliciously
in anticipation, as I
slowly slide open the
drawer with your name.

Bare flesh beneath a
sanitary white sheet.
Skin like porcelain,
slightly blue.

My sutures hold you together,
like a child's baseball
left behind on a sandy lot.
Cool lips cover
clear mortician's wax
hiding wires deep
beneath.

Pink eye-caps, when removed
corneas reflect my image
standing naked by your
side.

Poets say love is eternal,
but we have precious few hours.
Tomorrow you belong to the dirt.
Food for carnivorous worms.

Tonight we do the dance macabre
while the moon is still high.
Come the morrow we bow our heads
and commence grave undertakings.

APOTEMNOPHILIA

BY DEBORAH L. DAVITT

The soldiers in the rehab ward,
fresh-fitted with graphite limbs,
grimaced as the orderly passed them by,
as he did every day—

always speaking such admiring words,
as he massaged their stumped limbs,
a glitter in his eyes, a fervor,
as if they were his possessions—

a little *too* much interest,
something too close to hunger
and they turned their faces away,
many refusing to speak,
as they tried to mend their minds
as well as their bodies.

They learned to balance anew,
trained recalcitrant flesh
to work with mechanical limbs,
trained their minds to understand
the input provided by a bionic gaze,
computer chips plants in their brains.

The worst off, grateful for exoskeletons
that let them walk and fight once more,
prepared to return to the meat-grinder of the war, but
were shocked when their orderly
claimed a spot in the bed next door.

He'd had his healthy limbs cut away,
had himself fitted for
arms and legs of graphite,
servomotors and bioelectric circuits.

"At last, I can be just like you," he said,
hunger still plain in his voice—

but every man and woman there
turned their eyes from him.

THE TEMPTRESS

BY RISSA MILLER

Real evil doesn't dwell in the shadows.
It asserts more than enough beauty
to draw you under,
to hold you loosely,
until you don't want to go.
Real evil is seduction
not mangled with fright.
She tastes as sweet as a thousand souls,
all of them coiled on her tongue
singing the loveliest song of temptation.
And you can decide
to follow,
to give her everything.
Love is paramount to the pain:
a catastrophe that plunges into the experience of living.
She feels you yearn for tenderness.
Everyone understands this need—
they have known it, missed it, dreamed of it, healed from it.
But when real evil comes, will you fall for it?
Will you enter her mouth,
taste of eternal ardor,
give her everything,
trade your soul
for her lovely lips?
Or will you stay behind...
wishing once more
for soft hands to tuck you
into the shabby bottom of the world,
tummy roaring with hunger?

RELEASE

BY SUSAN MUSCH

I come for you
I am the unseen slow burn in the back of your throat
Heaviness in your eyelids
Weariness in your core
Your head aches for me
You tremor for me

I come for you
I am of the menacing earth
Of ancient beasts and monsters
Crude and organic
You forged me with heat as hot as Jupiter's fires
Molding and shaping me for diurnal pleasures

I come for you
You never planned for my emergence
A spark, a lapse, releases me
From the lake of fire of Gehenna
Deconstructing ordinary life into molten ash
I slip free of your vessels
Hydrocarbon estoiles fly through cerulean sky
Your careless inattention summoned me
So now

I come for you
You sit waiting
Sheltering in place
From what you created.

REGARDING ME

BY MICHAEL H. HANSON

At night it is regarding me,
before I sleep it peeks to see
that I have not fled or escaped
the favor of its scrutiny.

Spying from cracks of deep shadow
I sense that it can somehow know
that I have felt its existence
in ways others mostly outgrow.

After warm dusk, but before night
between the realms of dark and light
it squirms and oozes between walls
of undulating ebon fright.

Awake it cannot get to me,
asleep I nestle oh so free
but traveling from wake to dream
vulnerable near syncope.

I do not know just what it wants
and if it merely likes my haunts
though I suspect chicanery
and dread a sudden dark response.

Perhaps it seeks to enter me
and wear my flesh like bourgeoisie
until exhausted it gets bored
of embracing crass revelry.

Or does it want to rape my mind
and make my very spirit blind
so that I might awake a ghoul
shunned and chased off by all mankind.

Sometimes I think I hear it breathe,
impatient to begin its siege
of my meager mortal borders
with all of its rapacious teeth.

CONJURING MONSTERS

BY MONICA S. KUEBLER

Maybe I conjure monsters
out of broken souls
with too much talent and too much pain.

Maybe I conjure hunchbacks and zombies
and things that go bump
then scream long into the night
because all I see is promise, is hope,
is the dream of something that is not this.

I don't see the scars, the cracks,
the way that wild woman danced on your back
and broke you.
I don't see the maniac who lurks behind your eyes,
threatening to snap at any misplaced phrase.
I only see the genius of what could be.

So maybe I don't conjure monsters,
maybe monsters conjure me.

ABOUT THE EDITOR

Stephanie M. Wytovich is an American poet, novelist, and essayist. Her work has been showcased in venues such as *Weird Tales, Gutted: Beautiful Horror Stories, Fantastic Tales of Terror, Year's Best Hardcore Horror: Volume 2,* and *The Best Horror of the Year: Volume 8, as well as many others.*

Wytovich is the Poetry Editor for Raw Dog Screaming Press, an adjunct at Western Connecticut State University, Southern New Hampshire University, and Point Park University, and a mentor with Crystal Lake Publishing. She is a member of the Science Fiction Poetry Association, an active member of the Horror Writers Association, and a graduate of Seton Hill University's MFA program for Writing Popular Fiction. Her Bram Stoker Award®-winning poetry collection, *Brothel,* earned a home with Raw Dog Screaming Press alongside *Hysteria: A Collection of Madness, Mourning Jewelry, An Exorcism of Angels, Sheet Music to My Acoustic Nightmare,* and most recently, *The Apocalyptic Mannequin.* Her debut novel, *The Eighth,* is published with Dark Regions Press.

Follow Wytovich on her blog at http://stephaniewytovich.blogspot.com/ and on twitter @SWytovich.

ABOUT THE JUDGES

Christa Carmen's work has been featured in *Fireside Fiction, Year's Best Hardcore Horror*, and *Tales to Terrify*, among other publications. Her collection, *Something Borrowed, Something Blood-Soaked*, is available now from Unnerving, and won the 2018 Indie Horror Book Award for Best Debut Collection. You can find her online at www.christacarmen.com.

Cynthia (Cina) Pelayo is the author of *Loteria, Santa Muerte, The Missing*, and *Poems of My Night*. She is an International Latino Book Award winning author, and an Elgin Award nominee. She is represented by Amy Brewer at Metamorphosis Literary.

ABOUT THE POETS

QuerusAbuttu or "Dr. Q." is an award-winning author and U.S. Navy veteran. While serving as a Forensic Nurse and Women's Health provider in the military she earned her MFA in Writing Popular Fiction at Seton Hill University and completed her Ph.D. in Public Health. Dr. Q. writes dark tales that often center around environmental destruction and various forms of violence. She works for the government by day and is a writer, poet, anthologist and editor at Scary Dairy Press LLC at night and on weekends. Dr. Q. is the author of the novel *Sapient Farm,* and has several short stories published in anthologies like *Mother's Revenge, Terror Politico* and *Hazard Yet Forward.* She lives in the wilds of Virginia where she hunts down feral phantoms and makes their stories her own. Follow Dr. Q. on Twitter @Querus_Abuttu, on Instagram at https://www.instagram.com/querusabuttu/and on her Facebook Author page at DrQAbuttu. You can find her work on her Amazon.com Author page: https://www.amazon.com/Querus-Abuttu/e/B009NDJ2RM She shares occasional thoughts or a free story or two on her author webpage www.querusabuttu.com . Stop by any time!

Colleen Anderson is a Canadian author writing fiction and poetry and has had over 150 poems published in such venues as *Grievous Angel, PoluTexni, The Future Fire, Heroic Fantasy Quarterly* and many others. She has performed her work before audiences in the US, UK and Canada and has placed in the Balticon, Rannu, Crucible and Wax poetry competitions. Currently she is working on two poetry collections. Colleen also enjoys editing and co-edited Canadian anthologies *Playground of Lost Toys* (Aurora nominated) and *Tesseracts 17,* and her solo anthology *Alice Unbound: Beyond Wonderland,* was published in 2018. *A Body of Work* was recently published by Black Shuck Books, UK. Living in Vancouver, Colleen keeps an eye out for mold monsters and mermaids. www.colleenanderson.wordpress.com.

Michael Arnzen holds four Bram Stoker Awards® and an International Horror Guild Award for his disturbing (and often funny) poetry, fiction and literary experiments. He has been teaching as a Professor of English in the MFA program in Writing Popular Fiction at Seton Hill University since 1999. To learn more about his writing, seek out the books Proverbs for Monsters or 100 Jolts, which collect the best of it to date. To see what he's up to now visit gorelets.com or follow him on twitter @MikeArnzen where he routinely posts news, oddities and random tidbits of terror.

Michael Bailey is a freelance writer, editor, book designer, and a resident of forever-burning California. He is the recipient of the Bram Stoker Award® (and 7-time nominee), Benjamin Franklin Award, over two dozen independent accolades, and a Shirley Jackson Award nominee. Publications include the composite novels *Palindrome Hannah* and *Phoenix Rose*, two short story and poetry collections, *Scales and Petals* and *Inkblots and Blood Spots*, a limited two-novelette collection called *Oversight*, the standalone novelette *Our Children, Our Teachers*, and a children's book of fables called *Ensō*. Edited anthologies include *Pellucid Lunacy, Qualia Nous, The Library of the Dead, You Human, Adam's Ladder,* four volumes of *Chiral Mad*, and the forthcoming co-edited anthologies *Prisms* and *Miscreations: Gods, Monstrosities, and Other Horrors*. He recently finished a memoir called *Seven Minutes* about surviving one of the most catastrophic wildfires in history (which he wrote in twenty-three days), as well as *Psychotropic Dragon* (a psychological thriller), *The Impossible Weight of Life* (a fiction collection), and in his spare time he is finishing *Seen in Distant Stars* (a horrific, dystopian, science fiction thriller). When he is not writing, editing, or slowly dying inside, he works as a Developmental Editor for an undisclosed publisher. Find him online at nettirw.com, facebook.com/nettirw, or @nettirw.

Carina Bissett is a writer, poet, and educator working primarily in the fields of dark fiction and interstitial art. Her short fiction and poetry has been published in multiple journals and anthologies including *Hath No Fury, Gorgon: Stories of Emergence, Mythic Delirium, NonBinary Review,* and the *HWA Poetry Showcase Vol. V.* She teaches online workshops at The Storied Imaginarium and she is a graduate of the Creative Writing MFA program at Stonecoast. Her work has been nominated for several awards and she was the recipient of the 2016 HWA Scholarship. Link to her work can be found at http://carinabissett.com.

Robert Payne Cabeen is a screenwriter, artist, purveyor of narrative horror poetry, and now a novelist, with his Bram Stoker Award winning debut Cold Cuts, from Omnium Gatherum. His screenwriting credits include *Heavy Metal 2000,* for Columbia TriStar, Sony Pictures, *A Monkey's Tale,* and *Walking with Buddha.* Cabeen's illustrated book, *FEARWORMS: Selected Poems,* was a 2015 Bram Stoker Award® nominee. As creative director for Streamline Pictures, Robert helped anime pioneer Carl Macek bring Japanese animated features, like *Akira* and dozens of other classics, to a western audience. Cabeen received a Master of Fine Arts degree from Otis Art Institute, with a dual major in painting and design. Since then, he has combined his interests in the visual arts with screenwriting and storytelling for a broad range of entertainment companies including Warner Brothers, Columbia/TriStar, Disney, Sony, Universal, USA Network, Nelvana, and SEGA. Robert is a City of Lost Angels native. He resides in the Miracle Mile with his wife Cecile Grimm. Together, they spawned three offspring—all smarter, better looking and more talented than he is—but certainly not as scary. For more about Robert Payne Cabeen, visit: robertpaynecabeen.com .

Robert Catinella is a Weird Horror author from the Boston area. He and his wife live by a babbling brook in the woods. By day, he is a mild-mannered Acoustical Engineer and Sonar Array manufacturer. By night, he is a serial hobbyist who has been varying things including a beekeeper, a cook, a FIRST Robotics mentor, and a wine maker.

G. O. Clark's writing has been published in *Asimov's, Analog, Daily SF, Tales For The Camp Fire Anthology*, and many other venues. He's the author of 14 poetry collections, the most recent, *The Comfort Of Screams*, and 2 fiction collections, *Twists & Turns* published in 2016. He's been a Bram Stoker Award® finalist, and was an *Asimov's* Readers' Award winner in 2001. He lives in Davis, CA in a mobile home entertained by books, cds, streaming TV, and fading dreams. See http://goclarkpoet.weebly.com for details.

Frank Coffman is a retired professor of college English, Creative Writing, and Journalism. He has published poetry, fiction, and scholarly research across a variety of speculative genres including the supernaturally weird and horrific, fantasy, science fiction, and adventure. A member of the Horror Writers Association and the Science Fiction and Fantasy Poetry Association, he has published a chapbook, *This Ae Nighte, Every Nighte and Alle: 33 Poems of the Weird, Horrific, and Supernatural* (July 2018); his *magnum opus* in speculative poetry, *The Coven's Hornbook & Other Poems* (January 2019, Bold Venture Press); and, on a more traditional note, *Khayyám'sRubáiyát: A New Version in English Verse* (June 2019, also from Bold Venture). In more scholarly writings, he has published essays on fantastic and imaginative fiction in general, but, specifically, work on the literary achievements of Robert E. Howard. He selected, edited, introduced, and did commentary for his *Robert E. Howard: Selected Poems*.Coffman might be called a "New Formalist" when it comes to his poetry, which is, almost exclusively, rhymed and metered verse. Although he believes that, "really, there is nothing 'new' about Formalism in poetry. It was backgrounded for a century or so by the rise of the *verslibre* movement, but this oldest form of poetry—actually oldest across all of the world's cultures—has never gone away." His favorite form is, without doubt, the sonnet, but, along with that form's many incarnations, his work experiments and innovates broadly across many cultures and poetic forms.

Nicole Cushing is the Bram Stoker Award® winning author of *Mr. Suicide* and a two-time nominee for the Shirley Jackson Award. Various reviewers have described her work as "brutal", "cerebral", "transgressive", "taboo", "groundbreaking" and "mind-bending". *Rue Morgue* recently included Nicole in its list of *13 Wicked Women to Watch*, praising her as an "an intense and uncompromising literary voice". She has also garnered praise from Jack Ketchum, Thomas Ligotti, and Poppy Z. Brite (aka, Billy Martin). Her second novel, *A Sick Gray Laugh*, will be released August 27, 2019 by Word Horde. A stand-alone novella, *The Half-Freaks* (published by Grimscribe Press) will appear in October 2019. Nicole lives and works in Indiana.

Deborah L. Davitt was raised in Reno, Nevada, where she graduated from UNR in 1997. While an undergraduate, she focused heavily on medieval and Renaissance literature from *Beowulf* to Shakespeare. She received her master's degree in English from Penn State, but found work as a technical writer on projects ranging from nuclear ballistic missile submarines to NASA to computer manufacturing. She currently lives in Houston, Texas, with her husband and son. Her poetry has received Pushcart, Rhysling, and Dwarf Star award nominations; her fantasy and science fiction short stories have appeared in *InterGalactic Medicine Show, Pseudopod,* and *Galaxy's Edge*; and her novels are available through Amazon. For more about her work, including her forthcoming poetry collection, *The Gates of Never,* please see www.edda-earth.com.

Stephanie Ellis writes dark speculative fiction and has been published in a variety of magazines and anthologies, the most recent being Nosetouch Press, *The Fiends in the Furrows* anthology and Demain Publishing's Short Sharp Shock Series with *Asylum of Shadows*. She is co-editor and contributor at *The Infernal Clock* and co-editor of *Trembling With Fear,* HorrorTree.com's online magazine. She is an affiliate member of the HWA. She has also gathered together her dark poetry and twisted nursery rhymes in the collection *Dark is my*

Playground, available on amazon. She has written two novels, one folk horror and the other post-apocalyptic industrial horror, both of which are currently seeking publication. Follow her at https://stephanieellis.org and on Twitter @el_stevie.

Timothy P. Flynn is a dark poet from Massachusetts. His previous poetry resides in *Space and Time* magazine, Anthocon's book collections: *Anthology Years 1-3, Wicked Tales, haikuniverse, Haiku Journal* and the *HWA Poetry Showcase Vol 5*. He is a member of the New England Horror Writers and an Affiliate member of the HWA. Follow him on Twitter: @TimothyPFlynn or on Instagram: instagram.com/timothypflynnwriter .

Poems by cataloging librarian **Adele Gardner** (www.gardnercastle.com) have placed in the Rhysling Awards (SFPA), Balticon Poetry Contest, and Poetry Society of Virginia Awards. With 46 stories and 249 poems published, her horror works appear in multiple anthologies by Flame Tree Publishing, Popcorn Press, and Raven Electrick Ink, as well as numerous Halloween issues and more. Adele is literary executor for her father, mentor, and namesake, Dr. Delbert R. Gardner.

Owl Goingback has been writing professionally for over thirty years, and is the author of numerous novels, children's book, screenplays, magazine articles, and short stories. He is a Bram Stoker Award® Winner, a three-time Bram Stoker Award® Nominee, a Nebula Award Nominee, and a Storytelling World Awards Honor Recipient. His books include *Crota* (Bram Stoker Award® Winner), *Darker Than Night* (Bram Stoker Award® Nominee), *Evil Whispers, Breed, Shaman Moon, Eagle Feathers,* and *The Gift*. Owl's short story collection *Tribal Screams* was published as a limited run in 2016, and recently republished to a much larger audience. The Coffee Shop of Horrors created an Owl Goingback's Tribal Screams roasted chestnut flavored coffee to tie-in with the collection. Owl was also one of eight writers chosen for DC Entertainment's 2016 Talent Development Workshop, and recently added comic book writer to his professional resume. His newest novel, *Coyote Rage*, was published in 2019. In addition to writing under his own name, Owl has ghostwritten for Hollywood celebrities—including a science fiction novel for a multiple Emmy Award winning actor. Owl also served in the United States Air Force, owned a restaurant/lounge, and worked as a cemetery caretaker.

Michael H. Hanson has written four collections of poetry: *Autumn Blush* and *Jubilant Whispers* (both published by Racket River Press), and *Dark Parchments: Midnight Curses and Verses* and *When the Night Owl Screams* (both published by MoonDream Press). He has written and sold numerous individual poems to various periodicals, magazines, anthologies, and online venues. Michael is the Creator of the Sha'Daa shared-world action/fantasy anthology series currently consisting of *Sha'Daa: Tales of The Apocalypse, Sha'Daa: Last Call, Sha'Daa: Pawns, Sha'Daa: Facets, Sha'Daa: Inked*, and *Sha'Daa: Toys*, all published by MoonDream Press. He has written and published over 100 short stories in the fields of science fiction, fantasy, and horror.

Amanda Hard is a former journalist and professional dancer. Her short fiction has appeared in numerous magazines and print anthologies, and her poetry has been published in two volumes of the *HWA Poetry Showcase*. She earned her MFA in fiction writing from Murray State University in 2018 and now lives in the cornfields of southern Indiana with her husband and son.

Freelance writer, novelist, award-winning screenwriter, editor, poker player, poet, biker, roustabout, **Travis Heermann** is a graduate of the Odyssey Writing Workshop, a member of the Authors Guild, an Active member of SFWA and the HWA, and the author of *The Hammer Falls, The Ronin Trilogy, Rogues of the Black Fury,* and co-author of *Death Wind.* His short fiction appears in anthologies and magazines such as *Apex Magazine, Alembical,* the *Fiction River* anthology series, and Cemetery Dance's *Shivers VII*, and others. As a freelance writer, he has contributed a metric ton of work to such game properties as *Firefly Roleplaying Game, Legend of Five Rings,* EVE Online, and *BattleTech.* He enjoys cycling, collecting martial arts styles and belts, torturing young minds with otherworldly ideas, and monsters of every flavor, especially those with a soft, creamy center.

Naching T. Kassa is a wife, mother, and horror writer. She is Head of Publishing for HorrorAddicts.net, an assistant at Crystal Lake Publishing, and a member of the Horror Writers Association. She lives in Eastern Washington with her husband, Dan, their three children, and their dog.

EV Knight writes horror and dark fiction. Her debut novel, *The Fourth Whore,* will be published in 2020 by Raw Dog Screaming Press. EV's short stories can be found in *Siren's Call* magazine and the upcoming anthology *Monstrous Feminine* from Scary Dairy Press. She is also cohost of the podcast *Brain Squalls with Knight and Daigh.* She enjoys all things macabre; whether they be film, TV, podcast, novel, short story, or poetry. She lives in the cold northern woods of Michigan's Upper Peninsula with her family and their two hairless cats.

Monica S. Kuebler is a contributing editor at *Rue Morgue* magazine, author of *Rue Morgue Library #3: Weird Stats and Morbid Facts*, and co-producer of the Great Lakes Horror Company podcast. She also writes poetry and monster stories, and has spent the last seven years serializing her young adult vampire series - which kicked off with *Bleeder (Blood Magic, Book 1)* - at Wattpad.com.

Curtis M. Lawson is an author of unapologetically weird and transgressive fiction, dark poetry, and graphic novels. His work ranges from technicolor pulp adventures to bleak cosmic horror and includes *Those Who Go Forth Into the Empty Place of Gods, Black Pantheons,* and *It's a Bad, Bad, Bad, Bad World.* Curtis lives in Salem, MA where he hosts the Wyrd Live Horror reading series.

Gerri Leen lives in Northern Virginia and originally hails from Seattle. You can find her poems in such places as: *Eye to the Telescope, Star*Line,Dreams& Nightmares, Eternal Haunted Summer,* and others. She also writes fiction in many genres, primarily fantasy—both light and dark, and often centered around mythology—and science fiction. Visit http://www.gerrileen.com to see what else she's been up to.

Lisa Lepovetsky has published more than 150 short stories and poems in dozens of magazines and anthologies,, such as *Cemetery Dance* and *HWA Showcase IV* and *V.* She earned her MFA from Penn State and has taught for them and the U of Pittsburgh for years. She writes and hosts mystery theaters as It's A Mystery! She has published a novel, *Shadows on the Bayou,* and a volume of dark poetry, *Voices from Empty Rooms.*

Author-Illustrator-Poet **Lori R. Lopez** has two sons, four cats, and many hats. Learn about her books at fairyflyentertainment.com. Titles include *The Dark Mister Snark, Leery Lane, The Witchhunt,* and Elgin-Nominated *Darkverse: The Shadow Hours.*

Donna Lynch is a Bram Stoker Award®-nominated horror author and the co-founder, lyricist, and singer of the dark electronic rock band Ego Likeness. Her works include the novels *Isabel Burning* and *Red Horses,* the novella *Driving Through the Desert,* and numerous poetry collections, *Daughters of Lilith,* and the Bram Stoker Award®-nominated *Witches* (Raw Dog Screaming Press) being among them. Her 7th poetry collection, *Choking Back the Devil,* will be released by RDSP in July 2019. Lynch lives in Maryland with her husband and collaborator, artist and musician Steven Archer.

Pete Mesling lives in Seattle, WA, surrounded by the natural beauty of the Pacific Northwest. Of course, night falls even there, and it is from both sides of this coin that Pete draws his inspiration. He reads broadly, travels when necessary, and flirts with pessimism at every opportunity.

Publishing highlights include *None So Deaf*, an acclaimed collection of short fiction; *All-American Horror of the 21st Century, the First Decade: 2000 - 2010*, in which he shares a table of contents with a cast of luminaries too lengthy to include here; and *Dig Two Graves, Volume 2* (forthcoming from Death's Head Press). Pete is also the official Clive Barker proofreader for Gauntlet Press, from *Everville* onward. This is his second *Poetry Showcase* appearance. Keep up to the minute on Pete's writing at www.petemesling.com, or seek him out on Twitter, Facebook, and Instagram.

When endeavoring any creative work, **Rissa Miller** is sharply aware both light and dark coexist in all life. Her home city of Baltimore, with its gritty telltale heart, is the perfect backdrop for her mix of poetic beauty and pain. Rissa's latest work explores negative emotions, blended with real and imagined monsters, all wrapped up in the alluring being of a temptress. This poem is the introduction of the temptress character in her upcoming book, *The Devil's Boudoir*. Rissa studied writing at New York University/Tisch School of the Arts and photojournalism at Western Kentucky University. When she takes breaks from writing, Rissa finds her way to regional theater performances, wanders local woodsy trails, bakes vegan cupcakes, gives haunted history tours, and loves getting lost in libraries. Almost always, there is a cup of green tea in her hand. She is Senior Editor at Vegetarian Journal magazine.

Lisa Morton is a screenwriter, author of non-fiction books, and award-winning prose writer whose work was described by the American Library Association's *Readers' Advisory Guide to Horror* as "consistently dark, unsettling, and frightening". She is the author of four novels and nearly 150 short stories, a six-time winner of the Bram Stoker Award®, and a world-class Halloween expert. Her most recent book, *Ghost Stories: Classic Tales of Horror and Suspense* (co-edited with Leslie Klinger) received a starred review in *Publishers Weekly*, who called it "a work of art". Lisa lives in the San Fernando Valley and online at www.lisamorton.com.

Lee Murray is a two-time Bram Stoker Award® nominee and New Zealand's most awarded writer of horror and weird fiction (Sir Julius Vogel; Australian Shadows). New to poetry, she is better known for her Taine McKenna military thrillers, and for the supernatural crime-noir series *The Path of Ra* (co-authored with Dan Rabarts). Lee lives with her family in the sunny Bay of Plenty where she conjures up stories and poems from her office overlooking a cow paddock. You can find her at https://www.leemurray.info/ and she tweets @leemurraywriter

Susan Musch is a Lifetime Member of the Gulf Coast Chapter of the Poetry Society of Texas where she has been Vice President for the past five years. In 2018 Susan received Top Honors in the Friendswood Public Library Ekphrastic Poetry Competition. Susan earned degrees in Spanish and Accounting from Lamar University and a Doctor of Jurisprudence from the University of Houston.

David Powell writes full-time in Georgia, though his day jobs have run the gamut from studio musician to farmhand. He seeks out the little pockets where things whimsical, dreadful, or pitch-black hide. He is a member of the Horror Writers Association and has published in *Grue, Near to the Knuckle, Yellow Mama, Black Petals, Shotgun Honey*, and *Calliope*.

Saba Syed Razvi, PhD is the author of the Elgin Award-nominated collection *In the Crocodile Gardens* (Agape Editions) and the collection *heliophobia* (Finishing Line Press), which appeared on the preliminary ballot for the Bram Stoker Award® for Superior Achievement in Poetry, as well as the chapbooks *Limerence& Lux* (Chax Press), *Of the Divining and the Dead* (Finishing Line Press), and *Beside the Muezzin's Call & Beyond the Harem's Veil* (Finishing Line Press). Her poems have appeared in several literary journals, as well as in anthologies such as *Carrying the Branch: Poets in Search of* Peace, Voices *of Resistance: Muslim Women on War Faith and Sexuality, The Loudest Voice Anthology, The Liddell Book of Poetry, Political Punch: Contemporary*

Poems on the Politics of Identity, The Rhysling Anthology, The Machine Dreams Zine, HWA Poetry Showcase, and *Dreamspinning*. Her poems have been nominated for the Elgin Award, the Bettering American Poetry Awards, The Best of the Net Award, the Rhysling Award, and have received a 2015 Independent Best American Poetry Award. She is currently an Assistant Professor of English and Creative Writing at the University of Houston in Victoria, TX, where in addition to working on scholarly research on interfaces between contemporary poetry and science and on gender & sexuality in speculative and horror literature and pop-culture, she is writing new poems and fiction.

Terrie Leigh Relf is on staff at Alban Lake Publishing where she handles special projects, which includes being the contest judge and editor for the semi-quarterly drabble contest. She is also the poetry editor for Tales from the Moonlit Path. In addition to being a published fiction writer and poet, Relf is also a life and writing coach. You can learn more about here at https://tlrelf.wordpress.com/

Suzanne Reynolds-Alpert writes science fiction, horror, dark fantasy, and the occasional poem. Her short fiction had appeared in the anthologies *The Final Summons, Killing It Softly (Vol.1)*, and *The Deep Dark Woods*. Read her poetry in the anthology *Wicked Witches*, the websites Tales of the Zombie War, Eternal Haunted Summer, and Strong Verse; and in *The Wayfarer: A Journal of Contemplative Literature*. She published a short collection of poetry, *Interview with the Faerie (Part One) and Other Poems of Darkness and Light* in 2013. Suzanne is a freelance content creation expert and editor with degrees in communication and sociology. She writes in between driving her kids around and meeting the incessant demands of her feline overlords.

WC Roberts lives in a mobile home up on Bixby Hill, on land that was once the county dump. The only window looks out on a ragged scarecrow standing in a field of straw and dressed in WC's own discarded clothes. WC dreams of the desert, of finally getting his first television set, and of ravens. Above all, he writes, and has had poems published in *Shock Totem, Strange Horizons, Apex, Space & Time Magazine, Big Pulp, Star*Line*, and others.

Peter Adam Salomon's debut novel, *Henry Franks*, was published by Flux in 2012. His second novel, *All those Broken Angels*, published by Flux in 2014, was nominated for the Bram Stoker Award® for Superior Achievement in Young Adult fiction. Both novels have been named a 'Book All Young Georgians Should Read' by The Georgia Center for The Book. He founded both National Dark Poetry Day (Oct. 7) and the annual international Horror Poetry Showcase for the Horror Writers Association. His short fiction has appeared in the Demonic Visions series among other anthologies, and he was the featured author for *Gothic Blue Book III: The Graveyard Edition*. He was also selected as one of the Gentlemen of Horror for 2014. His poem 'Electricity and Language and Me' appeared on BBC Radio 6 performed by The Radiophonic Workshop. Eldritch Press published his first collection of poetry, *PseudoPsalms: Prophets* (nominated for the Elgin Award), and his second and third poetry collections, *PseudoPsalms: Saints v. Sinners* and *PseudoPsalms: Sodom* (nominated for the Elgin Award), were published by Bizarro Pulp Press. In addition, he was the Editor for the first books of poetry released by the Horror Writers Association: *Horror Poetry Showcase Volumes I* and *II*. He is a member of the Society of Children's Book Writers and Illustrators, the Horror Writers Association, the Science Fiction & Fantasy Writers of America, the Science Fiction Poetry Association, the International Thriller Writers, and The Authors Guild.

David Sandner is a writer and scholar of the fantastic, including horror, sf, and fantasy. The novelette, *Mingus Fingers*, co-written with Jacob Weisman, is forthcoming Fall, 2019 as a book from Fairwood Press. Recent work came out in online horror magazine *Dissections*, fantasy magazine *Space and Time*, and horror anthology *D.O.A. III*. You can also find work archived online at *Mythic Delirium* and

PodCastle. He has published in *Asimov's*, *Pulphouse*, *Fields of Fantasy*, edited by Rick Wilber, *Tails of Wonder and Imagination*, edited by Ellen Datlow, *Baseball Fantastic*, edited by W.P. Kinsella, and more. He is a 2014 Mythopoeic Award Finalist for scholarship on the fantastic. He is editing a scholarly collection, *Philip K. Dick. Here and Now*, forthcoming Fall, 2019. He is a Professor of English at California State University, Fullerton. Check out his online archives, including the Philip K Dick in the OC website and the Frankenstein Meme website, and his own site: davidsandner.com.

E. F. Schraeder is the author of two poetry chapbooks, most recently *Chapter Eleven* (Partisan Press). Schraeder's work has appeared in *Birthing Monsters, Mobius: The Journal of Social Change, Mystery Weekly Magazine, The Feminist Wire*, and other journals and anthologies. Schraeder's studied applied ethics and the humanities in graduate school and holds an interdisciplinary Ph.d. in social philosophy. Current projects include a queer monster's coming of age novella and a full length manuscript of poems.

Ann K. Schwader's poems have recently appeared in *Spectral Realms, Dreams & Nightmares, Star*Line, Weird Fiction Review*, and *Modern Haiku*. Her most recent poetry collection, *Dark Energies* (P'rea Press 2015) was a Bram Stoker Award® Finalist, as was one previous collection, *Wild Hunt of the Stars* (Sam's Dot 2010). She is also a two-time Rhysling Award winner, for both short and long form speculative verse. In 2018, she was chosen as an SFPA Grand Master. Ann lives and writes in suburban Colorado.

Marge Simon lives in Ocala, Florida and serves on the HWA Board of Trustees. She has three Bram Stoker Awards®, Rhysling Awards for Best Long and Best Short Fiction, the Elgin, Dwarf Stars and Strange Horizons Readers' Award. Marge's poems and stories have appeared in *Clannad, Pedestal Magazine, Asimov's, Silver Blade, Bete Noire, New*

Myths, Daily Science Fiction. Her stories also appear in anthologies such as *Tales of the Lake 5, Chiral Mad 4, You, Human* and *The Beauty of Death*, to name a few. She attends the ICFA annually as a guest poet/writer and is on the board of the Speculative Literary Foundation.

John Claude Smith has had four chapbooks, three collections, and two novels published, including the Bram Stoker Award® finalist *Riding the Centipede.* He is currently working on a novel, a novella, short stories for anthologies, and a play, the latter with his girlfriend, the poet/editor/translator, Alessandra Bava. He splits his time between the East Bay of Northern California, across from San Francisco, and Rome, Italy, where his heart resides always.

Christina Sng is the Bram Stoker Award®-winning author of *A Collection of Nightmares* (Raw Dog Screaming Press, 2017). Her work has appeared in numerous venues worldwide and received nominations in the Rhysling Awards, the Dwarf Stars, the Elgin Awards, as well as honorable mentions in the *Year's Best Fantasy and Horror* and the *Best Horror of the Year.* Visit her at http://www.christinasng.com and connect on social media @christinasng.

Chad Stroup received his MFA in Fiction from San Diego State University. *Secrets of the Weird,* Stroup's debut novel, is available from Grey Matter Press and his second novel, *Sexy Leper,* is available from Bizarro Pulp Press. His short stories have been featured in anthologies such as *Chiral Mad 4, Lost Films, Splatterlands, and California Screamin',* and his dark poetry has appeared in all previous volumes of the HWA Poetry Showcase. Follow him on Instagram (@chadxstroup), and drop by his Facebook page at https://www.facebook.com/ChadStroupWriter.

Anna Taborska is a British filmmaker and horror writer. She has written and directed two short fiction films, two documentaries and an award-winning TV drama. She has also worked on twenty other films, with actors such as RutgerHauer, Scott Wilson, Noah Taylor and Jenny Agutter, and was involved in the making of two major BBC television series: *Auschwitz: the Nazis and the Final Solution* and *World War Two behind Closed Doors—Stalin, the Nazis and the West*. Anna's short stories have appeared in over thirty anthologies, including *Best New Writing 2011*, *The Best Horror of the Year Volume Four* (2012), *Best British Horror 2014* (2014), *Year's Best Weird Fiction Volume 1* (2014) and *Nightmares: A New Decade of Modern Horror* (2016). Anna's debut short story collection, *For Those who Dream Monsters*, published by Mortbury Press in 2013, won the Dracula Society's Children of the Night Award and was nominated for a British Fantasy Award. Anna's other books include *Shadowcats*—a mini-collection of cat stories published by Black Shuck Books in June 2019, and *Bloody Britain*—a collection of short stories and novelettes due out soon from Shadow Publishing. You can watch clips from Anna's films and view her full résumé here: https://annataborska.wixsite.com/horror

Sara Tantlinger resides outside of Pittsburgh on a hill in the woods. She is the Bram Stoker Award®-winning author of *The Devil's Dreamland: Poetry Inspired by H.H. Holmes*. She is a poetry editor for the *Oddville Press*, a graduate of Seton Hill's MFA program, a member of the SFPA, and an active member of the HWA. She embraces all things strange and can be found lurking in graveyards or on Twitter @SaraJane524 and at saratantlinger.com .

Ingrid L. Taylor is a speculative fiction writer, poet, and veterinarian. She lives in the desert with a black cat, a Newfoundland dog, and several hummingbirds. Her stories have appeared or are forthcoming in *Red Rock Review*, *Dies Infaustus*, *Legs of Tumbleweed*, *Wings of Lace: An Anthology of Literature by Nevada Women*, *Gaia: Shadow and Breath, vol.3*, and others. In 2018, she was awarded the HWA Dark Poetry Scholarship and a Playa artist residency. She is currently completing a science fiction novel set in the Southwestern United States as well as a collection of dark poetry. Follow her on Instagram @tildy_bear for pictures of her animals and updates on her writing.

Mary Turzillo's poetry collection, *Lovers & Killers*, won the 2013 Elgin Award. Her 1999 Nebula winner,"Mars Is No Place for Children," is read on the International Space Station. She has been on the British SF Association, Pushcart, Stoker, Dwarf Stars, and Rhysling ballots. *Sweet Poison*, written with Marge Simon, was a Bram Stoker Award® finalist and won the 2015 Elgin. Her novel *Mars Girls* came out in 2017 from Apex. *Bonsai Babies,* a collection of literary horror, was published by Omnium Gatherum in 2016. *Satan's Sweethearts,* also with Simon, won second place in the Elgins. Her current project is *A Mars Cat and his Boy*. Mary was on the US foil fencing team for Veteran World Championships in Germany, 2016. She lives in Ohio, with scientist-writer Geoffrey Landis.

Trisha J. Wooldridge writes short stories, novellas, novels, articles, and poetry about bad-ass faeries, carnivorous horses, social justice witches, vengeful spirits—and mundane stuff like food, hay-eating horses, social justice debates, writer advice, and alcoholic spirits. Her more recent stories and poems can be found in *Wicked Haunted*; *Darkling's Beasts and Brews*; *Nothing's Sacred Volume 4; HWA Poetry Showcase Volume 5*; the Blackstone Valley Artist Association Art-Poetry shows of 2017, 2018 and 2019; and in the upcoming *Wicked Weird* and *Twisted Book of Shadows* anthologies. She's recently joined The Writer's Ally and has edited over sixty novels and four anthologies. As child-friendly T.J. Wooldridge, she's published poetry, three spooky children's novels, and will be part of HWA's upcoming *New Scary Stories to Tell in the Dark* (HarperCollins 2020). She's a member of SCBWI, HWA, New England Horror Writers, New England Speculative Writers, and Broad Universe. She spends rare moments of mystical "free time" with a very patient Husband-of-Awesome, a calico horse, and a bratty tabby cat. Join her adventures at www.anovelfriend.com.

Marty Young is a Bram Stoker Award® nominated and Australian Shadows award winning writer and editor, and sometimes ghost hunter. He was the founding President of the Australasian Horror Writers Association from 2005-2010, and one of the creative minds behind the internationally acclaimed *Midnight Echo* magazine, for which he also served as Executive Editor until mid-2013. Marty's first novel, the award-winning *809 Jacob Street*, was published in 2013. His short fiction has been nominated for both the Australian Shadows and Ditmar awards, reprinted in an Australian year's best anthology, and repeatedly included in year's best recommended reading lists. Marty's essays on horror literature have been published in journals and university textbooks across the world, and he was also co-editor of the award winning *Macabre; a Journey through Australia's Darkest Fears*, a landmark anthology showcasing the best Australian horror stories from 1836 to the present. His website is www.martyyoung.com

www.ingramcontent.com/pod-product-compliance
Lightning Source LLC
Chambersburg PA
CBHW020318130626
46549CB00003B/921